Pikmi to Be Your Valentine!

Written by
Meredith Rusu

SO CUTE

SCHOLASTIC INC.

ISBN 978-1-338-31606-3

10 9 8 7 6 5 4 3 2 1   18 19 20 21 22

Printed in the U.S.A.   40

First printing 2018

Book design by Becky James

It was Valentine's Day in Pikmi Land. The Pikmis decorated the trees and bushes with lollipops and candy hearts. Everyone loved Valentine's Day!

4

But no Pikmi loved Valentine's Day more than Ollie.

Each year, Ollie surprised a special Pikmi with a lollipop rose and asked, "Will you be my valentine?"

Of course, picking just *one* valentine was hard. Ollie had lots of friends!

"If I pick Fancy, we could spend the whole day sliding down rainbows," Ollie thought. "Or if I pick Leroy, we could split an extra-yummy banana split."

The other Pikmis wanted to be Ollie's valentine, too.

"I hope Ollie picks me!" said Bibble. "Ollie is woolly wonderful."

"I hope Ollie picks me! Picks me!" chimed in Chata.

"Ollie can't pick all of us," Fuwa pointed out. "You can only have one valentine on Valentine's Day."

What would the Pikmis do?

Then Fuwa got an idea!

"We'll each give Ollie a gift. The Pikmi with the best surprise will be Ollie's valentine!" Fuwa said.

The Pikmis loved Fuwa's plan.
They started to get popping!

11

Chata made Ollie a Valentine's Day card.

Tater was going to dig a hole for Ollie, but decided to string charms into a golden friendship bracelet instead.

Chata found Ollie first.

"Happy Valentine's Day!" the parrot squawked. "Here's a card for my bestie! I hope you pick me to be your valentine!"

"What a sweet surprise!" said Ollie. "Thank you, Chata!"

Then Fancy popped up from behind a tree.
"I made you yummy heart cakes!" Fancy said.
"Please be my valentine."

"Wow," said Ollie. "Thank you! These treats are melting my heart!"

17

As the day went on, Ollie got more and more gifts.

Outside, Ollie saw Tater.

"Here is a golden charm bracelet for a golden friend!" said Tater.

19

Ollie couldn't believe how amazing all the Pikmis were.

"But now I'm really in a Pikmi pickle," Ollie said. "Everyone is being so kind. I feel bad picking just one friend."

Suddenly, it started to rain heart-shaped banana peels from the sky.
Leroy soared overhead!

"You're the pick of the bunch!" Leroy shouted through a megaphone. "Please pick me to be your valentine, Ollie!"

Before Ollie could answer, a sweet melody started playing. It was Bobble singing a Valentine's Day song.

"You're the greatest friend I know," Bobble sang.

"You two have lifted my spirits sky-high," Ollie said. "Thank you both!"

All the Pikmis gathered for the Valentine's Day celebration. Everyone wanted to see whom Ollie would pick.

Then Ollie took the microphone onstage. Ollie had a surprise box.

"I love Valentine's Day," Ollie said. "But what I love even more is having friends like you. I pick . . ."

Then Ollie opened the box and gave each Pikmi a lollipop rose!

"A valentine is supposed to go to the Pikmi who makes you feel the most special. But you all make me feel special," Ollie said.

Everyone cheered!

"So," said Ollie. "I guess it's my turn to ask. Will you *all* be my valentine?"

"Yes, Ollie! Yes!" the Pikmis shouted.

After all, nothing is more special than celebrating Valentine's Day with your best Pikmi friends!

From:

_____

From:

_____

From:

_____

From:

_____